Was My Face Red

Words by
Judith Conaway

Pictures by
Katie Maloney

Raintree Editions

© 1977 by Raintree Publishers Limited

Last week I went to a party at Aaron's house.
My mother thought it was a fancy birthday party.
So she made me wear my long yellow dress. I
didn't really want to dress up like that. But
Mom said all the kids would be in party clothes.

Was she wrong! All the kids were there — Aaron, Cathy, Mitchell, and Neil. They all had on play clothes. I was the only one who was dressed up! All the kids laughed when they saw my dress.

Was my face red! I really felt stupid. I looked so different from all of them. I knew they would tease me about my dress for days and days. All I wanted to do was go somewhere and hide.

But, after a while, the kids were pretty nice about it.

"Don't worry, Rachel," said Aaron. "I know just how you feel. I hate it when people make me dress up. Last year I went to my cousin's wedding, and you know what? My aunt made me get my hair cut the day before the wedding. The man did a terrible job. My hair looked awful. I had to go to the wedding like that! Boy, was my face red that time!

"Once I got a new pair of glasses for reading. They were big and thick and ugly. I just hated those glasses. Every time people saw me in those glasses, they would laugh. I wanted to run and hide my face."

"You looked pretty funny," said Neil. "I could have died laughing!"

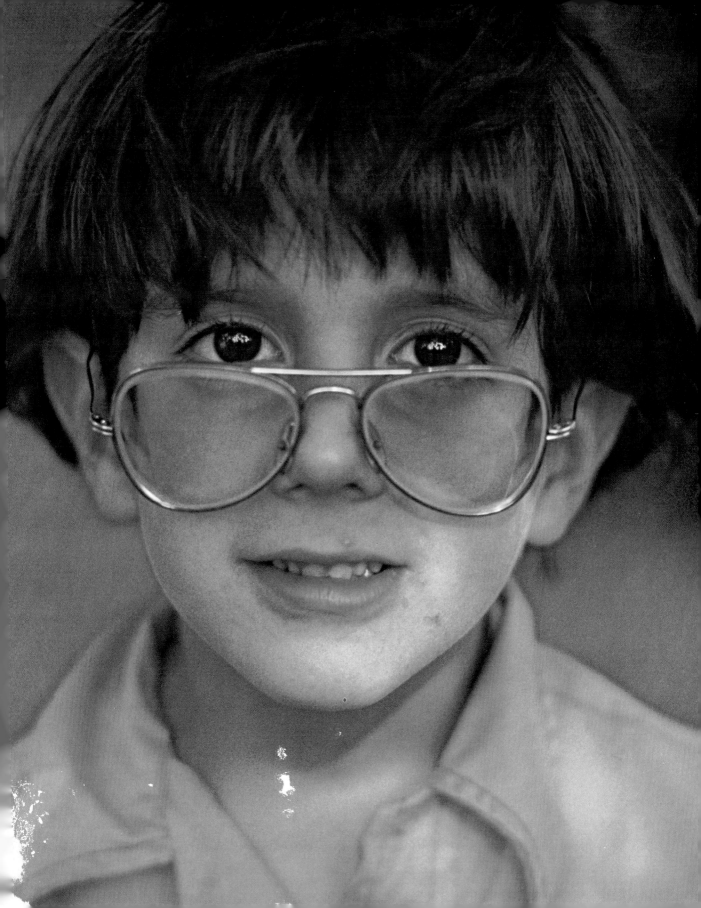

"Well, what about the garbage can, Neil?" asked Aaron. "Tell them about that."

"Oh, all right," Neil said. "It was like this. There was a fence that I wanted to climb. It was right next to some garbage cans. I was in a hurry. As soon as I stepped on the lid, I felt my feet start to slip.

Sure enough, I landed right in the garbage. Ugh, that was awful. It was so smelly. I knew Mom would get mad when she saw my clothes. And the worst thing was that Cathy and Aaron heard the crash. They came out from their house. They saw me in the garbage can. They must have laughed for a whole hour. I could have died."

"Do you know what else happened to me?" asked Aaron. "I was climbing a fence. Just as I lifted my leg over, I heard a noise. *R-r-r-i-p!* I looked back. And — you guessed it — it was my pants!

"One time I made a bet that I could eat a whole hot dog in one mouthful," said Neil. "I made the biggest hot dog I could. It had chili, tomatoes, catsup, everything. But when I tried to eat it, the stuff spilled out of the hot dog. It went all over my clothes. Was my face red!"

"I got really embarrassed once," said
Mitchell. "It was my report card. I almost
always get an A in science, but last time
I got a C. I was worried. I didn't want to
show my dad. I was sure he would be mad.

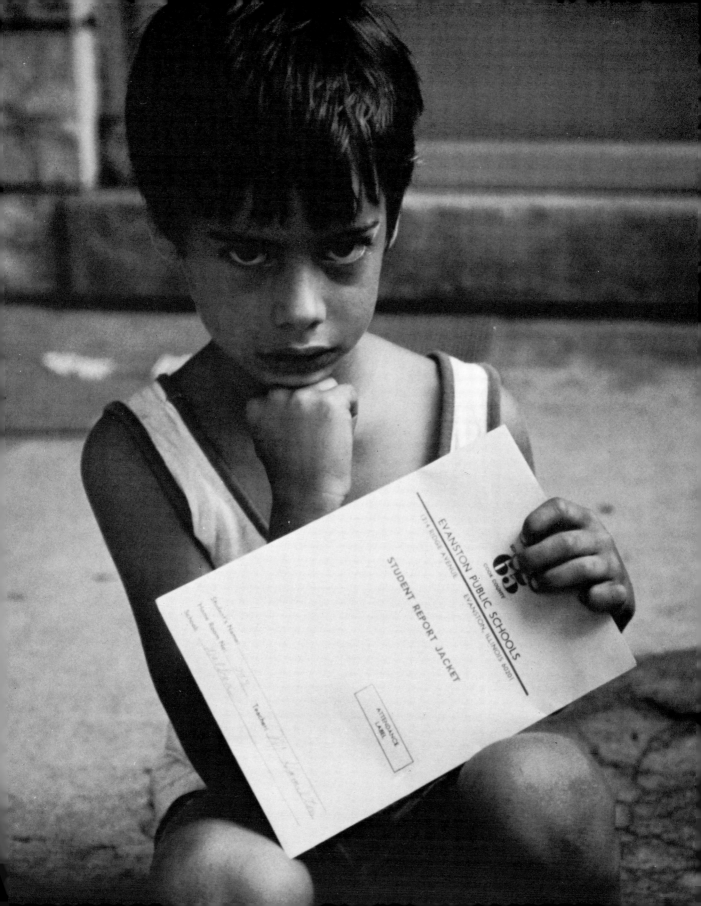

Then Cathy saw me and asked me what was the matter. I showed her the report card. She told me not to worry. Then she kissed me. I guess she was trying to make me feel better. But when sisters kiss you, it makes you feel stupid. You know what I mean?"

"Hey," said Cathy, "do you know what happened to Mike, the big kid down the block? Someone pinned a tail on him when he wasn't looking. He walked around like that for over an hour. People would look at him and laugh. But he didn't know why they were laughing. Finally I told him about the tail. Was his face red!"

Everyone laughed at Cathy's story. But I thought the person who pinned the tail on him was pretty mean. It isn't any fun to be embarrassed. I bet Mike didn't think it was very funny.

The party at Aaron's house turned out to be fun after all. What the other kids said really helped. I guess everyone does silly things once in a while. Everyone feels embarrassed sometimes.

Something funny happened later at the party. I saw Aaron walking around with his hand over his mouth. I asked him what was the matter. He really turned red. Then he showed me. He had fallen and lost a tooth. He didn't want anyone to see how funny he looked.

"Don't worry, Aaron," I said. "I understand just how you feel."

I smiled.

And after that, Aaron forgot about his tooth, and I forgot about my dress. We all had a very good time.